Retaliation

Retaliation

Elaine Ricks

For more information, contact: elaineelaine350@gmail.com

Character Information

Teresa Williams a.k.a. Envy - age 32, housewife, low self-esteem, quiet, and perfect.

Twins - 3 years old boy and girl (Names – Justin and Justice)

Abused mentally

Mother talks about her outside appearance (weight)

Only child

No family except immediate

High school drop out

Married to Richard for 14 years

Richard Williams - age 32, construction contractor, mellow, and sneaky.

No family

Works sufficiently and travels for his company

Married Teresa after high school

Clean cut dresser

Teresa is getting breakfast ready for her family. Richard came downstairs, getting ready to sip his decaf coffee, and indulge in his steak and eggs, until his cell phone rang. He answered it and said, "Hello...Sorry, I am running late...Yes, I am on my way with the contracts." He hung up and turned to his wife, "Honey, I am sorry I will have to take a rain check on breakfast." He kissed the kids on the forehead and kissed Teresa on the lips. He picked up his briefcase and dashed for the door.

Teresa said, "Come on kids. Finish up your breakfast so you all can be the first faces Ms. Miller sees in her class."

Teresa dropped off the twins and said to herself, "Oh no, I am running late for the meeting."

Teresa made a sharp turn into Hillsbury Estate, where she is the president of the Lady's Hillsbury Association. When Teresa finally got there, she was greeted by the snooty women of Hillsbury. She began to start her presentation on the community service project she created, when she received a text message from her husband explaining to her what time he was getting off and what he needed her to do.

Text message: Hey honey, I get off at 2 o'clock. I need you to pick up my clothes from the cleaners and I know you've been wanting to buy something for the house. So, pick out some new furniture for the living room that you like. I know you've been asking for some. Also, we will talk about where you want to go for your birthday. I know you wanted Chinese, but I feel like eating fish. Love you.

Teresa rushed in a panic and hurried to complete her meeting and all the tasks her husband asked of her. She looked at the time and it said 1:30. She was supposed to pick up Justice and Justin from day care at 1 o'clock. She finally made it to the daycare center and picked the twins up. After picking the twins up, she ran into the house and began cooking. When she finally gets Justice and Justin settled down so they can take a nap, she heard Richard's personal phone he left at home go off. She saw a message. She said to herself, "Check, don't check." She ended up checking and it was nothing. She heard Richard's car in the driveway and immediately put the phone back where she found it.

Richard rushed into the house just to say, "Honey, I have to leave. Something important has come up."

Teresa said, "What is more important than spending time with your family?"

"Money I make. That's what keeps this family together."

"No amount of money can keep me away from you," said Teresa.

Richard began to play with Justice and Justin. Justice said, "Daddy, you smell like mommy's perfume."

"Yes, this is because I gave mommy a big hug and a kiss."

Teresa smiled and said to herself, "Yes that's mommy's perfume, but mommy stopped wearing it two months ago."

Teresa said, "Okay kids, it is time for me to give you all your bath so you can take a nap." Teresa gave the twins their bath and put them to bed.

Two hours later, Richard finally made it back from helping his female friend fix her flat on her car. He looked at Teresa and said, "I'm going to take a shower and go to bed. I have a big day tomorrow."

"Okay dear. I will come to bed later," she replied.

Richard went upstairs and said to himself, "Man, that was close."

Teresa finally went up to get ready for bed. After she was in bed, she looked at Richard and frowned at him.

Richard's phone went off and he had it on vibrate but what he didn't know was that Teresa was not asleep. She was still thinking about earlier that day with the perfume. Richard looked over at Teresa to see if she was still asleep. Teresa felt him looking at her, so she closed her eyes.

Richard answered the phone and said, "I thought I told you not to call me when I'm at home. I will talk to you tomorrow," and hung up the phone.

Richard woke up early the next day for work. Teresa got the twins up for breakfast. Usually, Richard sat down at the table to eat breakfast with the family. He looked at Teresa and said, "I need you to take some money out of our account. I want you to have a girl's day at the spa with your friends."

Smiling, Teresa said, "This brings back so many memories."

Richard was at the office reviewing some contracts. His secretary Tammy walked into the office and told him she made reservations at the restaurant Frenchez. Richard told Tammy, "Thanks, and here are the contracts. I will be leaving early."

Richard got into his car to go home and get ready for his date with Teresa.

Teresa told the twins to put their books away while mom and dad get ready for their date. The doorbell rang and it was Angie the babysitter. Teresa opened the door and said, "You're early. I have food in the oven for the twins."

Richard came out in his black three-piece suit.

Justin said to his dad, "You look nice."

Justice ran up to her dad and tried to hug him.

Richard said, "Oh babies, you're going to get daddy dirty."

Teresa came upstairs. The twins said, "Mommy, you look pretty," and they ran and gave her a hug.

She said, "Thank you babies. Mommy and daddy are going to be out for a little while, so make sure you listen to Angie."

Richard and Teresa walked out the door. Richard got to the car and opened the door for Teresa.

Teresa said, "Thank you dear."

Richard got in the car and Teresa said, "You know we have not been out in a while like this."

"I know dear. I have just been so busy working I haven't had time for you and the kids like I should."

At the restaurant, the hostess said, "May I help you?"

Richard said, "We have reservations for Williams."

The hostess led them to their table. Richard pulled the chair out for Teresa. Teresa said, "Thanks dear."

"You are welcome."

The waiter came over to the table and said, "Are you ready to place your order?"

Richard replied, "Yes, we would like two side salads, two T-bone steaks, and for dessert, we would like your famous apple pie with whip cream."

Teresa said to Richard, "This is so nice. We need to do this more often."

"Yes, we do need to do this more."

The waiter repeated the order to them and added a bottle of house wine Shayeen 1918. Teresa said, "Thank you so much."

Richard said, "Baby, you look so good in that black dress. I can't wait to get you home and tear that dress off with my teeth."

Teresa smiled at Richard as he continued eating. She looked into Richard's eyes, and he looked into hers and she said laughing, "I was thinking the same thing."

They returned home a couple of hours later, checked on the kids, and paid the sitter. They were so impressed with the sitter that they let her know that they would be calling her again.

Richard took off Teresa's clothes with his teeth. Teresa took off Richard's clothes. She told her husband he needed to put on a condom. He responded with, "Not tonight. I know what I'm doing."

She told him, "I'm not trying to get pregnant."

Richard said, "I am not trying to get you pregnant either, just lay back and enjoy the ride."

They began to make passionate love. After they finished, they both looked at each other and smiled. Richard told Teresa, "I see you really missed me."

She smiled and said, "I see you miss it too." They kissed and went to sleep.

The next morning, Teresa got the twins up and started to prepare breakfast. Richard came down the stairs and smiled at Teresa. She smiled back. Justin said, "What's funny mom and dad."

Richard said, "Nothing, eat your breakfast."

Teresa asked Richard, "Are you eating breakfast with us this morning?"

"No dear, I need to get to the office early," Richard replied. Richard gave Teresa and the twins a kiss.

Teresa told the twins to get their books for school. She dropped the kids off and returned home. She began to clean up and prepare dinner. Richard's second phone started vibrating again. She told herself she wasn't going to answer, walked away, and continued to clean. She took the kids' clothes upstairs. She noticed the phone vibrating again. She looked at it and answered. "Hello," and no response. She sat down and said, "Who could that have been? I know Richard isn't cheating on me."

She left to get the kids. Meanwhile, in the back of her head she said, "Maybe they had the wrong number."

Later, they arrived at home and Justin and Justice asked if they could have a snack. She told them to wait until after they ate their dinner first.

Richard called Teresa and said, "Dear, I am going to be a little late. I'm trying to finish the contracts at the office."

"Ok, your food will be in the oven." Teresa fed the twins and gave them their bath. She read them a bedtime story and they both fell asleep. Teresa took her bath and tried to stay awake for Richard. She fell asleep only to wake up and find that it was 12 o'clock at night and Richard was not home. She called Richard's office. No answer. She called his cell, and it went straight to voice mail.

Richard walked in and warmed up his food. Teresa went downstairs and asked Richard, "Where have you been?"

Richard answered with, "Honey, I closed on a big account today. We went out to celebrate. The team and I."

"Why didn't you call? I was worried about you."

"I lost track of time dear, sorry. Hey, have you seen my other phone? I think I misplaced it."

"Yes, it's on the dining room table."

"Thanks babe."

Teresa went back upstairs to bed.

Richard finished up his dinner and went up the stairs and took a shower. Teresa laid across the bed thinking to herself, "What is going on?"

Richard got out of the shower and put on his pajamas. Teresa said, "Babe, I'm ready. Let's make love."

"Baby, I'm tired, maybe tomorrow."

Teresa said, "Yeah right."

"What did you say babe?"

Teresa said nothing. Richard received a phone call at 8 o'clock in the morning. He told Teresa that it was a client that they were trying to get. He had to go out of town to get the contract signed. Teresa said, "I'm tired of you having to leave us all the time."

Richard said to Teresa, "If you want to keep living like this, you shouldn't get tired of me going out of town."

"It's just that me and the kids miss you when you're gone."

Richard hugged Teresa and said, "Babe, I miss you all too but this is what I have to do." Richard headed upstairs to pack his clothes.

Teresa said, "Ok dear."

The twins ran up to their dad and asked if they could go with him. Richard said, "Not this time."

Teresa hugged Richard with an attitude. Richard looked at her and said, "I love you all."

The twins asked Teresa if they could go to the park and play. Teresa said, "It's too early kids, maybe later."

Richard made it to Ann County and called Teresa to let her know he arrived safely. He told her he had to meet with one of the top bosses to get the contract signed and would call her back later.

Teresa said, "Ok," with an attitude.

There was a knock at Richard's door. It was a stripper he met at a gentlemen's club the last time he was in Ann County. Richard said, "Come in. I've been waiting on you."

She said, "I've been waiting for you to come back in town," and closed the door smiling.

The twins said, "Mommy, are we going to the park?"

"My head is hurting."

"You said later and it's later."

"Not now."

"But you said later mommy." The twins started crying and ran to their rooms.

Teresa went into the room and said, "I'm sorry babies. I will take you to the zoo tomorrow." She went into her room and laid down. She woke up running to the bathroom to vomit. She called Richard to tell him how sick she had been feeling.

Richard answered, "I hope you are not pregnant," as he was laughing.

Teresa said, "That's not funny."

"Maybe it was something you ate."

"I'm going to the doctor to see if something is wrong."

"Come on baby, you are alright. It was something you ate."

Teresa called the doctor to get an appointment and the nurse said he had a cancellation that day.

Teresa said, "Okay," and dropped the kids off at school and headed to the appointment.

Character Information

Lisa Jackson a.k.a. Ivy - age 40, Bible school teacher, and outgoing personality.

No Children

Impressive dresser

Her mother, sister, and father are in ministry

Master's in Theology

Married for twenty years

Met husband in her father's church

Father introduced them

Vincent Jackson - age 45

Pastor

No Children

Nice dresser wears mainly suits

Helps the community

Organizes church events

Married for twenty years

Vincent preached, "Whatever's in the dark comes out in the light. You cannot hide anything from God. He knows what you are going to do before you know. Can I get an amen? Whatever you have done in your life, whether good or bad, you will have to answer to the Great One and God is going to reveal your secrets. There is nothing you can hide from the Great One. I mean nothing. So, if you don't have your life together, get your life together. Can I get an amen?"

There were sounds of praises unto our God. "And now would there be anyone who would like to let go and let God take the wheel?"

His wife came up to take the names of 6 people who received God as their savior. His wife shouted, "Thank you Jesus," and hugged her husband.

Church ended and everyone gathered outside to greet and give thanks to their minister for the wonderful sermon. Sister Odell said to pastor Vincent, "Thanks for that wonderful sermon."

Sister Michelle said, "Pastor, I need you to come and pray for me."

"What's wrong Sister Michelle?"

"I need you to pray for my back, so I can start back working out, so I can get my sexy back together for my third husband," she said smiling.

"I'm going to pray that God heals your back."

Lilly interrupted, "Yes, healing is always the answer."

Pastor Vincent turned in disgust and headed toward his office. He made sure that the door was locked. He hung up his robe, dimmed the lights, and immediately began to check his email. All of sudden, there was a knock at the door. He answered and was greeted with a kiss on his lips from his wife. "That was a wonderful sermon, pastor. I'm on my way to the grocery store to get something to prepare for dinner. Is there anything you want in particular?"

"No, honey, it is your decision. I'm sorry that I have a very important email I need to read. I will meet you at the house in about an hour." He kissed Lisa on the cheek and shut the door.

Lisa stood and looked at the closed door in astonishment. She said to herself, "Lisa, you are just trying too hard." Lisa got into her car, diving away in her white Cadillac.

While she left the church parking lot, Vincent looked at her out of his office window. His heart was racing as he burst into a sweat and said to himself, "Not now Lisa. Not now."

Everyone made it to Lisa and Vincent's house. Lisa and her mom were preparing dinner and said, "Where is Vincent? It's time for dinner."

Lilly said to herself, "At the GM Motel."

Lisa responded, "What did you say Lilly?"

"Oh nothing. I said I hope he's alright."

"Okay everyone, let's give Vincent about 10 minutes. If he is not here by then, we will start without him."

Five minutes later Vincent walked in. Lisa said, "Oh honey, I'm glad you made it. We were waiting for you."

Vincent replied, "Honey, I'm not feeling too good. Will you all go on and start without me. I am going to bed."

Before Lisa could say anything, Vincent dashed upstairs. Lisa said to herself, "What did I do this time?"

Lilly walked in the next room and started laughing to herself. Everyone finished eating and left. Lisa locked the door and cleaned up.

Lisa went upstairs and said, "Honey, is everything okay? Everyone was worried about you."

"Lisa, I am just tired. It has been a long day. Just give me a little time to take a nap." Vincent rolled over on his side.

The next morning, Lisa woke up to see her husband not in sight. This was very unusual because Lisa always woke up with her husband by her side. Lisa ran down the stairs calling for Vincent. There was no answer. When she called him again, he said, "Meet me in the living room."

She thought to herself, "Why the living room?" She looked at the time. It was 4 o'clock in the morning. There were rose petals on the floor, lit candles, smooth jazz music playing in the background, a fire in the fireplace, and red wine poured in nice wine glasses. Lisa said, "Oh Vincent, this is nice."

Vincent put his finger over her mouth and said, "Shhhh baby, I've been so stressed. I have been taking everything out on you. This morning, I am going to make it up to you first lady."

They began to dance to their favorite song. When they stopped dancing, Vincent began to make love to his wife. This was the first time he made love to her in a long time.

7

Three weeks later.

Lisa woke up with a really bad headache and Vincent said, "Are you okay?"

"I just feel really horrible. I'm going to take a couple pain pills and lay back down."

When she got up, she took a pregnancy test. When Vincent arrived home, she said, "Honey, we're going to have a baby." Vincent looked at her puzzled. "Finally, God has blessed us with a baby."

"How do you know that test is 100 percent right?"

"Because it is, and I also made a doctor appointment because I want the baby to be heathy."

A couple of hours later, Lisa got an emergency phone call from the church. She forgot about the first lady conference. She ran to take a shower. Lisa said to herself, "How in the world did I forget about this?"

Later that day, Lisa got ready to take care of her busy schedule with bible study for teenage girl's social retreat that they have at the church.

Lisa and Lilly ran into each other in the hallway. "Hi sis, how are you doing?"

Lisa said, "I'm doing wonderful."

"You have a glow about you."

"Well, me and Vincent made passionate love. It felt just like my wedding night, Lilly."

"I thought every time you all made love it was supposed to be passionate."

Lisa said, "Not really, Lilly. He needs to keep coming home late." They both started laughing. "Oh, I can tell I am the only woman."

Lilly whispered to herself, "If you only knew, you ARE the only woman," and started smiling.

"Well, I am about to go on this retreat with the girls."

"Ok, I am going to get lessons together for my bible class tonight."

Lisa thought to herself, "I'm really enjoying myself," as she got into the church van with the girls. "Okay, now let's have some fun today."

The girls shouted and yelled.

Lisa made it home from the retreat saying to herself, "Man, I am so tired. I know I am getting old, but I am not that old. Maybe it's because I am pregnant. Let me call my husband and see what time he will be home."

There was no answer. "That's strange. He always answers my calls. Maybe he is talking to a church member or something."

Vincent finally called back.

Lisa answered, "I have been trying to call."

"I know. Sorry, I've been working on my sermon for Sunday."

"Okay, just trying to see what my wonderful hubby wants for dinner."

"Whatever you cook, it is okay with me."

"What time will you be home?"

"We can eat dinner together in a couple of hours, okay?" He then thought to himself, "I don't know why she always calls and shows up at the wrong time. I mean I really hate that I got married. Now let me see what I missed on the chat. If this guy looks like he sounds, this is just what I am looking for. Someone that can put it down or let me put it down." He started laughing.

Vincent messaged, "Do you want to meet somewhere?"

"Yes," messaged the stranger.

"Okay, well I know this really nice motel on the other side of town called the Dew Drop Inn."

"I know where that is. It's off highway 93."

"Yes," replied Vincent.

"One thing you need to know is I don't take checks." Both started to laugh.

"See you in 15 minutes."

"You really move fast."

Vincent said, "That is the only way I move when I am meeting a sexy man like you."

Vincent finally made it home four hours later. "Man," saying to himself, "I'm going to call him back. He knows how to put it down. I am not even hungry." He walked up the stairs to take his shower and get ready for bed. He smiled and said, "That was so good."

Lisa woke up. "What did you say Vincent?"

"I said that food you cooked was good. Thank you, babe."

"I was trying to stay up so we could eat dinner together. I was so tried after that retreat with the girls."

8

Two weeks later

Vincent and Lisa sat in the living room together. Lisa said, "Vincent, I have been throwing up for a couple of days and I really think the test is right."

Vincent replied, "I thought we couldn't have any kids."

"You of all people know how God works."

"Well Lisa, just wait until you know for sure before you start jumping around the room, okay?

"You sound like you don't want a child."

"I do babe. I just don't want you getting your hopes up for nothing."

"Well, I called the doctor to see if he can get me in earlier than my appointment."

"Okay."

"Okay, Pastor Vincent? where is your faith?"

He said, "I am sorry. You're right," and hugged Lisa.

Lisa ran upstairs crying, saying to God, "What is wrong with him? He really has changed."

Vincent was still downstairs watching TV saying, "God, I hope she's not pregnant because I am really enjoying myself."

The next day, Lisa received a call from the nurse saying she could come in that day because the doctor had to go out of town the same day as her appointment.

Lisa said to Vincent, "I am on my way to the doctors. Are you going?"

"Yes, I guess. I am so sorry about last night. I know we serve a high and powerful God. I love you."

"I love you too."

At the doctor's office.

"Good morning, Pastor Vincent Jackson and First Lady Jackson. Just sign in and someone will be with you," said the receptionist.

Lisa said, "Okay," with a big smile on her face.

The nurse came to the door, "Mrs. Jackson, follow me." Once in the room, the nurse asked, "What are you here for?"

"We are going to have a baby. I took a pregnancy test and it said that I was pregnant."

"That's good! I know you and the Pastor have been trying for years to have a baby, but first things first, I need you to pee in this cup, okay?"

Lisa said, "I have the test with me."

"We can't use that because it's not always accurate."

Lisa said, "Okay."

"Lisa, I need you to come in this room and the doctor will be with you shortly."

"Okay."

The doctor walked in, "Hello Lisa Jackson, well you're not pregnant. The test shows negative. I am so sorry because I know you wanted a baby...maybe next time."

Lisa responded, "Why did the test say I was?"

"Let me see that test you have Mrs. Jackson. This test is a year old. It has expired.."

Lisa looked hurt with tears running down her face. "Why am I throwing up and having really bad headaches?"

"Let me run some tests. The nurse will be back in to take some blood. I will have your results in 24 hours."

Lisa walked out of the doctor's office with tears coming down her face.

Vincent asked, "What is wrong babe?"

"You were right. I am not pregnant."

Vincent hugged Lisa and said, "It's going to be alright."

"I am ready to go home."

Vincent took Lisa home. "Babe you can just relax today. I will ask your sister to teach the bible class today."

Vincent arrived at church. "Can I talk to you," he said to Lilly.

Lilly smiled and said, "You can talk to me anytime and anywhere."

"Please Lilly, I just need you to teach your sister's class today."

"Where is my sister? I thought the class was hers."

"She doesn't feel good today."

"What is wrong with her? You finally got it right this time?"

Vincent replied with an attitude, "She went to the doctor and why are you asking all these questions anyway. Are you going to do it or not?"

Lilly laughed, "Anything for my sister and you too, Pastor."

"Why do you talk to me like that? I am your brother-in-law and I am also your Pastor."

"Who were you with when I saw you coming out of the Dew Drop Inn?"

Vincent laughed, "That wasn't me. I am a married man. I will never cheat on my wife with another woman."

"I know," and Lilly walked away smiling.

9

"Hello?"

"This is Dr. Quencher's office. Your test results are in. Can you come in today?"

"What's wrong?"

"Mrs. Jackson, I can't tell you over the phone."

"Okay, let me put some clothes on. I will be there in an hour."

Lisa arrived at the doctor's office, "Hi, I am Mrs. Jackson. I was told to come in for some test results today."

"Have a seat Mrs. Jackson and someone will be with you shortly."

She then sat next to another woman, Teresa.

"Hello," said Teresa.

"Hey," Lisa replied.

"How are you doing?"

Lisa answered, "Well I came in today to see what was going on. They had me come in for some test results. The doctor did some blood work because I was feeling really sick. I thought I was pregnant. I took a pregnancy test, but the test was expired and gave a false reading. I didn't know it was expired until the doctor looked at it. I felt really silly."

"Well, I thought I was pregnant, and I have twins so what does that tell you about me. I am here also for blood work results."

"That's a blessing. Are you married," Teresa responded.

"Yes, to one of the most caring hardworking men I know. Are you?"

"My husband is Pastor Jackson. He is also a hardworking man of God."

The nurse was at the door, "Mrs. Williams, you can come back now. The doctor will see you. The room on your right is open."

Another nurse, "Mrs. Jackson you can come back now. The doctor will see you. The room on your left is open."

The doctor came in and sat down, "Mrs. Jackson how are you doing today?"

"Fine. I've just been kind of nervous because I don't know what is going on with me," Lisa replied.

"Well Mrs. Jackson, I don't know really how to tell you this."

"Tell me what doctor?" She panicked, "What is wrong with me."

"Well, your test shows that you have AIDS."

"What did you say? How could that be? I am married to a Pastor. He is the only one I have been with." She began crying and screaming, "No! no!"

"I need your husband come in a soon as possible."

"He's going to do more than just come in."

"We have better medicine now than 20 years ago. Here are some samples until you fill your prescription."

Lisa threw the medicine on the floor of the room and stormed out of the building.

Talking to the nurse, the doctor said, "Sometimes I hate my job."

"Well, you have one more."

The doctor went into Teresa's room, "Mrs. Williams I have your results from your blood work."

"What is wrong doctor? Is my sugar high again because me and the twins have been eating everything in sight."

"No, Mrs. Williams. I hate to tell you this, but you have AIDS."

"I have what? How?"

"Yes, I had the blood work double checked."

Teresa was shocked, "Can I get a second opinion because this can't be true. My husband is the ONLY man I have ever been with."

"You can if you like. If that will make you feel better. We send all our blood work to the best lab in the state. Until you do, I need to see your husband. Here are some samples until you get your prescription filled."

Teresa left the office crying, saying to herself, "Why me? Why me?"

Lisa was sitting in her car crying.

Teresa saw her, "What is wrong first lady? I was going to ask you to pray for me. I got my results, and it is bad."

"Well, I just got my results back to. This is why I am sitting in this car crying. Your results can't be as bad as my results."

"If I tell you first lady, you have to promise that you won't tell anyone," Teresa said.

"One thing you can do for me is don't ever call me first lady. I found out that I am not."

"Okay. My husband gave me AIDS and I know I didn't give it to him. I never cheated on him."

"Well, I just found out that Pastor Jackson has done the same thing. He runs around like he's trying to preach God's word, when he knows better than the men out here in this world. When I get home, I will find out what is going on." Lisa started crying, "I don't know what to do. My family. The church."

"When I get home, he has a lot of explaining to do and then he is getting out. He thinks I am quiet and that is why he did this, but he has another thing coming."

Both women exchanged numbers.

Lisa went to the church to see the Pastor. Everyone already left for the day. She stormed into his office and caught him on the internet. "Oh now, this is what you do when I am not around. I see why I got AIDS."

"You got what?" He was shocked.

"What? You heard me? Why are you on the internet? You trying to find someone to cheat with? You brought this mess into our relationship. I am not the one that's cheating. What is this? You telling this man that you want to get with him? You have messed up my life." With that, Lisa slapped the Pastor and ran out of the church.

Teresa finally made it home after driving around for three hours. Richard was at home with the kids because he didn't have to work. She walked into the living room. "What in the world have you been doing out here in these streets? You told me that you are out there making money for your family, but you been doing more than that. I want you out of my house."

"What are you talking about woman?"

"Oh, you don't know. I got my results back from the doctor and you gave me AIDS."

"I haven't given you anything. You might have given it to me."

The twins asked, "What is AIDS?"

"Go upstairs," Richard told them.

"You need to go right now before I do something to you that I am going to regret. Richard, your stuff will be on the porch."

"I am going to leave, but I will be back because I don't want the kids to see you and I argue."

"Just leave like you been doing. Go on another business meeting. You will hear from my lawyer. I am going to get you for everything you've got," and with that she threw a vase at Richard.

"I should have left you a long time ago," Richard said.

"Well, I wouldn't have AIDS." She slammed the door crying and ran up the stairs to her room.

10

One month later

The phone rings…Teresa thought, "I know this isn't Richard calling me." She answered the phone with an attitude, "What!"

Lisa was on the other end, "Are you okay?"

"I thought you were that no-good man of mine."

"I need to talk to you about something. I want to do something to get back at those no-good cheating men. I am so mad."

"What is it?"

Lisa said, "I will come over tomorrow after you drop the twins off."

"Yes, come about noon."

"Talk to you then."

The next day, Teresa dropped off the twins at daycare.

Lisa called Teresa and told her, "I'm on my way early."

Ding dong, ding dong.

Teresa answered the door.

Lisa was at the door, "Hey sis."

Teresa responded, "Hey, how have you been doing?"

"I guess as well as can be expected. Let's cut the small talk. What I came up with is that we can dress up in different wigs and clothes and go to all these clubs in the city because they don't know you and they don't know me. We can teach these no-good men a lesson."

Teresa liked the idea, "Okay, because I am so tired of these men out here doing their wives wrong. When are you talking about doing this?"

"As soon as possible. Have you heard from your husband?"

"Yes, but I just changed my number. What about you?"

"Yes, about a month ago. He told me he had changed and asked God for forgiveness. I just hung the phone up in his face and guess what I found out. My sister knew about it but didn't tell me. If she would have told me, I probably wouldn't be in this situation."

"Why didn't she tell you?"

"She wanted him. That is why."

"How do you know that?" Teresa asked.

"Because Vincent confessed to everything. That's why. Her husband is on my list. Let's talk about what we are going to do."

Lisa got up to leave and Teresa told her to call later.

Three days later, Lisa called Teresa. "What time are you coming over?"

"I will be over about 5 o'clock so you can have time to get ready."

"Well, I was going to call the babysitter to come over around that time."

Lisa arrived at Teresa's house. "You look good. You don't look the same."

"That is the point. You won't either when I get through with you. We are also going to change our names. Your name is going to be Envy."

Teresa agreed. "Lisa, what is your name?"

"Ivy."

"Why Ivy?"

"It's like poison Ivy."

"Why did you name me Envy?"

"Because they are going to envy everything you do," Lisa laughed.

Teresa laughed, "Well Ivy, let me kiss the kid's good night."

"Mommy, you look nice."

"Thank you, baby. I love you."

Lisa and Teresa went to the club Sensation. This was their first stop.

Lisa said, "Look at that guy and he is still wearing his ring. Good."

"Oh, you get that one."

"Let's get our drink on."

"I don't drink," Teresa replied.

"Me either, but I am going to drink tonight."

"Well, I will have one drink."

Lisa told Teresa, "I got the stuff in the car. I made overnight bags."

"What stuff Lisa?"

45

"The stuff we are going to need so we can do what we came out here for."

"What are you talking about Lisa?"

"I have some pills to put in their drinks when we are at the hotel. They can be knocked out. Why are you asking all these questions?"

"Because you didn't tell me how we were going to do it."

"I'm sorry. I was just thinking about my cheating husband. I also have some tombstones with the phrase 'Everything that looks good ain't good. AIDS.'"

A stranger walked up and said, "Hey, what's your name?"

"Ivy and Envy. What's your name?"

"James. Are you married?"

Envy replied, "No, but we see you are."

"Does it matter?"

Ivy said, "No, so what's up with you tonight?"

"The same thing that's up with you."

Envy said, "You call it, so let's go."

They made it to the hotel and Ivy already had a room.

"You girls know how to party?"

"Oh, we know. Sit back and relax while Envy makes us a drink."

"So, how do you like your drink?" Envy asked.

"It's pretty good."

"James, we are going to go in the bathroom so we can get ready for you."

Teresa and Lisa came out of the bathroom. He was very drunk and asked the ladies, "What did you put in my drink?"

They said, "Nothing."

Five minutes later, he was drowsy. Ivy took his clothes off, while Envy set up the props from the overnight bag. They both took turns on the man. They left the man at the hotel with an unopen condom on one side of him and the tombstone on the other side of him.

The next day they did the same thing. This was happening every weekend. The ladies were going to different clubs and targeting married men.

Teresa asked Lisa, "What I don't understand is why are you letting them know that we have the disease? Aren't you even a little scared?"

"No, I'm not. They need to keep their thing in their pants."

"What if they find out who we are, and they try to kill us?"

"You worry too much. That's why we changed the way we look, okay?"

"Well, I have kids to worry about. These men are not the ones that gave us this disease."

"Who knows, they might. My husband likes men," Lisa responded.

Lisa dropped Teresa off at home.

11

One week later, Lisa called Teresa.

"Hello," Teresa answered.

"How you doing today?"

"I am okay. How are you?"

"Are you ready for tonight?" Lisa asked.

"Ready as I'm ever going to be."

"I got you a new wig," Lisa laughed.

"What is so funny?"

"You are going to be a blonde tonight. You are going to look so sexy."

"What time Lisa?"

"The same time as always. See you later."

They made it to the club. "Hey Teresa, you see those two men right there?"

"Yes, Ivy." They both started laughing.

"Let's go get them, Envy."

"Hey, my name is Ivy, and this is Envy. What are your names?"

"Well, my name is Scott, and my friend is Jeff."

"Mmmm…"

"Why did you do that?"

"Because I like what I see."

"We do too, and we are looking for some fun. We have a room at the hotel around the corner. It's getting too crowded in here."

They left the club and went to the hotel.

Ivy asked, "What do you men want to drink?"

"Whatever you make for us."

"My kind of men."

Scott asked, "So are you girls married or have a man in your life?"

"We were, but not anymore."

"We'll toast to the fools that let you go."

Envy said, "I see you are married."

"Yes, we are, but we are not trying to hide it either. We see if a woman is going to do it or not. Hey, you make some strong drinks."

"I know. We are going to go to the bathroom to get ready," Ivy responded.

Jeff said, "That's what I'm talking about, but you can get ready right here," smiling.

Teresa and Lisa came out and both men were drowsy. They did the same thing to them as well. Teresa looked surprised.

Lisa asked her, "Why are you looking like that? You knew what we were going to do before you started."

"I know but I just don't understand why we keep letting them know. Okay, I don't like this. Just pass me two tombstones in that bag and two condoms, so we can get out of here. I have to get home to my babies."

Lisa dropped Teresa off at home.

"Did you have fun Mrs. Williams?" the babysitter asked.

"Yes, thank you again. I will be needing you every Saturday."
Thinking to herself, "Let me check on my babies. Man, this is
really scary what we're doing. I don't know if I am going to be
able to keep doing this." She started crying, "How could he do
this to me and the kids?"

12

Lisa, thought to herself, "I am going to get every man that is married smiling. I guess I will call Teresa."

"How are you doing Teresa? Are you okay?"

"I'm okay, just tired."

"You have some beautiful babies. I wish I had a child. I know there's really no hope for me," Lisa said crying.

"We are going to be alright. I will call you tomorrow."

The next morning, Teresa called Lisa.

"Hey Lisa, what are you doing?"

"Nothing let's go shopping so I can spend some of his money. I want to buy me some red bottom shoes. He would never let me buy them when I was with him, but I am going to get them now. I am going to need some more wigs for the weekend too."

Teresa and Lisa returned from shopping.

"I need to go pick up the twins."

"Oh, could I go with you? If that's okay."

"Sure, you can go with me."

After picking up the twins, Lisa said, "Well, I am going home. I am tired. I think it's that medicine making me feel this way."

"I get like that too sometimes."

"Okay, call you later."

Teresa looked at the twins, "So what do you and your sister want for dinner?"

Justin screamed, "Ice cream."

Teresa laughed, "No food? What about some old string beans, chicken, and rice?"

"If they old mommy, I don't want any."

Teresa laughed, "I don't mean like that. They aren't old."

"That is what you said mommy."

"Okay, well do you want some string beans, chicken, and rice?"

The twins responded, "Yes, can we play with our toys mommy?"

"Yes, I love you Justin and Justice."

"We love you too mommy."

The phone rang. Richard was on the other end, "Hey babe."

"Why are you calling me? Did you get the divorce papers? They were sent to your job."

"Not my job babe."

"Yes, your job and don't call here, okay? How did you get my new number anyway?"

He said, "Don't worry about that."

"Let this be your last time calling me. You need to try and find out who gave us this disease." Teresa hung up the phone.

Richard started crying and talked to God, "God, please forgive me. I am so sorry for not loving my wife. I should have. Please give me one more chance with my family. I promise I will do the right thing by them."

Teresa called Lisa, "Why Richard's no good behind call me. I told him don't call me again."

"He is lucky you haven't gone to his office."

"Right. I have been thinking about breaking all his car windows but that just makes me even more mad."

"I wouldn't break his windows but breaking his neck, that's what you should do."

"I have to think about the twins."

"He wasn't when he was out there with those women."

"What did you do when the famous Pastor was messing around with those men?" Teresa asked.

"Don't get an attitude with me."

"I know what you were saying, but I don't see you at the church doing anything."

"Just leave it alone, okay?"

"No problem."

"I just hope you are ready for tonight," Lisa said.

"Don't worry about me, are you?"

"Please, you the one scared, not me."

"Okay, let me call the babysitter."

"Okay, I will see you at 8 o'clock Envy."

"Okay, Ivy," both started laughing. "Justin and Justice, let's get ready for your bath."

"Mommy, you said we can have some ice cream after we ate those old string beans, chicken, and rice," Justice reminded.

"Mommy, you did," Justin jumped up and down.

"You're right, but after this you and your sister are going to bed."

"Okay."

Teresa said to herself, "Let me get ready before Lisa gets here."

The babysitter arrived, "Hello, Mrs. Williams."

"Hey, thanks again. I don't know what I would do without you."

"It's no problem."

"The twins have eaten, taken their baths, and are in bed."

The doorbell rang.

"Hey, Lisa. Let me get my coat."

"I'll be in the car."

"Are you ready?"

"Yes, Envy," as Lisa laughed out loud, "Oh, I'm sorry."

"You are so silly."

"I know, but you have to laugh to keep from crying."

"You are so right about that."

They went to another club

"Let's sit right at the bar, Envy."

"Okay. Ivy, look at that guy that's walking this way, but he's by himself."

"So, we can both act like we going to do him."

"Does he have a ring on his finger?"

"Most married men take it off."

"Oh!" exclaimed Teresa.

The man walked over to Lisa and Teresa. Lisa greeted him, "Hello!"

"Hey, how are you two beautiful women doing tonight?"

"Without," Lisa responded.

"'Without what?"

"Without a man," Teresa responded.

"Why is that?"

"Because we are in the middle of a divorce," Lisa stated.

"Divorce," repeated the man.

"Yes," Teresa confirmed.

"Well, this is better for me."

"Are you married?" Lisa asked.

"Well, we are going through something right now."

"We don't even know each other's name and we are just talking," Teresa said.

"My name is George."

"My name is Ivy, and this is Envy."

"Nice to meet you both."

"Well, I am glad you are going through something because we would have never met. What about we leave this club and go to our room."

"Okay, lead the way. Is your friend staying?"

"No, we do everything together if that's okay with you," Lisa said.

"Hey, the more the merrier," George laughed.

They made it to the hotel.

Envy reminded Ivy, "Don't forget the overnight bag."

"It is really nice to have a king size bed for all of us," Ivy said.

"I know," George replied.

"Just sit back and relax. We got this. I make some good drinks."

"Yes, she does," Envy replied.

"Here is your drink George and here is your drink Envy."

"This is a good drink Ivy. Thanks!"

"We are going to put on something a little more comfortable," Ivy told George.

"Man, this drink got a brother's head spinning. Do you need me to come in there with you all?"

"We got it. Just chill." Envy said to George. She turned to Ivy and said, "Let's turn the shower on so he can think we're taking a shower."

"You are really taking charge tonight."

"I know because this is going to be my last time doing this. We can talk about it later."

They both walked out of the bathroom.

"He is almost knocked out. Come on and you get on top of him first," Ivy said to Envy.

George woke up just a little to ask them what was going on.

"Nothing. Just making you feel good and pass back out."

"See that is what I mean," Envy said to Ivy.

"Leave the tombstone, unopen condom, and a black rose," said Ivy.

Teresa said, "Why a black rose?"

"I'm trying something different."

In the car, Lisa said, "You told me you were going to do my sister's husband. After him we will stop."

"Lisa, no more. This has to stop."

Lisa dropped off Teresa and sped away.

Teresa talked to God, "I've really messed up a lot of people's lives trying to get back at people that have not done anything to me. I am sorry. I know you are a healer and that's all I had to do was ask you for healing."

"Is everything okay Mrs. Williams? I heard you talking to someone," the babysitter asked.

"Yes, I was just talking to God."

"God is good, and he is also a healer. You just let go and let God take the wheel. The battle is not yours."

Teresa hugged the babysitter and started crying.

"It's going to be okay. Do you need me to stay the night with you?"

"I am going to be alright. I just got to do one more thing and I'll be okay. Here is your money. Thank you again."

13

A week passed by. It was Saturday night. The night Teresa had to do it one more time. She gasped for air as her heart raced. Just knowing the evil and preposterous things she was about to do. All of a sudden, she received a text message from Richard saying he wanted to start over and make everything right again. He also told her that he had changed his life and got saved. She had happy tears running down her face.

This was the one time she knew she was going to have a good relationship.

As soon as she started to text him back, she heard a honking noise. It was Lisa. Teresa kissed her kids on their forehead, said goodbye to the babysitter, and dashed for the door.

"What is wrong with you? I am tired of this attitude," Lisa told Teresa.

"Come on so we can get this over with."

"I thought we were in this together. I am starting to realize you are weak."

"I can handle this. Remember, you are the one that taught me everything I know," she rolled her eyes at Lisa. Teresa started to cry and said, "Lisa, we can get out of this?"

"You can get out of this, but I am just getting started Mrs. Envy."

They finally pulled up in front of the club. Lisa pointed at a tall bald head, dark skinned man. She said, "Now that is what I am talking about. I have the room at the Uptown Hotel, 103."

Teresa said, "Why that room number? That is the room I wanted."

Lisa laughed, "That's the number of men we infected," and drove away.

As soon as Teresa walked in the club, Lilly's husband spotted her. He began to ask questions, "Where are you from?"

"Croville. I own my own business." After two hours of talking, dancing, drinking, and sharing stories, Teresa invited him over to her room. Lisa already prepared the drinks for them. Teresa and Lilly's husband started to kiss. "I'll be right back. Don't do anything without me," Teresa started laughing.

Lilly's husband replied, "I won't."

By the time Teresa came out of the restroom, Lilly's husband was intoxicated. She performed a sexual number on him, as he was knocked out.

Lisa said, "Teresa, I'm going to miss you."

"I'm going to miss you too, keep in touch."

Lisa dropped Teresa off at her house and drove away. When Teresa returned home, she began to pray, repent and ask God to forgive her, save her soul, and to make her body's spirit clean again.

The next morning, Lisa went to the bank and cleaned out her and the pastor's bank account. Then she went to the church and got the money out of the safe. She left the country to get plastic surgery from a doctor who changes the identity of criminals.

14

One month later

Teresa pulled up in front of Michael's Restaurant, where she agreed to see Richard. Teresa gasped.

"Hello, sweetheart. You are looking good."

"Thanks!"

"I am really sorry for what I have done to this family. I want to make things work."

Teresa said, "Me too."

Just as Richard and Teresa kissed, George walked past and said, "Richard, what's going on." They shook hands. "This is my fiancé Veronica."

Richard said, "Hello, Veronica. Veronica, George this is my wife, Teresa."

George said, "Have I met you somewhere? You look awfully familiar."

Teresa said, "No, but you look familiar too."

The two couples sat down, and George talked about how much he appreciated Richard. How he stayed by his side when he didn't have anyone else.

Later on, the two couples departed after sharing stories. After Richard and Teresa left, George said to himself, "Where do I know you from miss lady. I don't forget a face."

15

It was family night at Lisa's house. Her mother, father, aunts, uncle, her husband's sister, and even Vincent was at home. The family was doing their usual line dance competition and family prayer.

Lisa's mom asked Vincent where Lisa was.

He responded, "I haven't talked to her or seen her since that night at the church."

Lisa's mom said, "What do you mean you haven't talked to your wife? What happened?"

"We're going through some things right now."

Lilly said laughing, "Maybe she realized you aren't the man she thought you were."

Lilly's mom told her, "Shut up. We're not going to have that foolishness in this house tonight. "

The family got ready to head into the living room to watch a movie when they heard the doorbell ring. There was a delivery guy with a package. Lilly said, "What is this?"

Lilly's mom said, "It is addressed to the family."

It was a flashdrive. Lilly's mom said, "What's on it."

When Lilly opened the file, there were sensual and sexual images of Lilly's husband and Teresa caught in action. The most disturbing thing was a tombstone on the side of Lilly's husband saying, "Everything that looks good ain't good," with an unused condom. The tombstone also said, "You have AIDS." The camera finally exposed the person with the video. It was Lisa laughing and yelling, "Sis, what goes around comes around."

16

Richard, Teresa, and the twins started going to church together, movies, trips, and lunch dates. They were trying to build their relationship and trust.

It was Mach 15th, the very first day they met. Richard told George that he was going to plan something special for his wife. He didn't know it was for the first time they met.

Later that day, while Teresa washed clothes, the doorbell rang. It was flowers and a card, "Meet me at the Anthony Hill. Suite 103. Love, Richard," with a key to the suite. Teresa immediately called her babysitter to watch the twins. She went shopping for a dress and a teddy. While leaving the house, she left her cell at home. She knew she didn't need it.

Around 6 o'clock, Richard returned from a long day at work and asked the babysitter, "Where's Teresa?"

The babysitter said, "She's supposed to be with you."

Teresa made it to the hotel. She opened the door to Suite 103. She said, "Honey, I'm here. Why are there so many candles in here? Didn't they pay the light bill (laughing) and why do you have black roses instead of red ones?" No one responded.

Richard told the babysitter, "No, I have been trying to call her all day on her cell."

The babysitter said, "Yeah, she left her phone, but you sent this wonderful bouquet of flowers and this card to meet you."

Richard read the card and said, "This isn't my handwriting."

"Then whose is it?"

"Oh my God, call the police."

Teresa heard footsteps from behind her. She said, "It's about time you showed up. I was getting worried."

As Teresa turned around, she realized the muscular image behind her was not Richard, but George. Teresa said, "George, what are you doing here? I am supposed to meet Richard."

George said, "Teresa, I am in disguise just like you were. Should I call you Envy?"

Teresa said, "I have changed."

George said, "I have to…." POP!

17

Seven years later.

Lisa was caught trying to cross the border. She didn't look the same because she had the plastic surgery. They were investigating the doctor she used for a long time. They had all the records and before and after pictures of the patients he performed surgery on.

The police told Lisa what happened to Teresa. Lisa said to the police that Teresa had asked her to stop, but she said, "I couldn't get past all the hurt and pain that was built up inside of me. All I could think about was retaliation against every man that ever cheated on their wife." She then said, "I know the battle wasn't mine. It was the Lord's. I pray that God forgives me for everybody's life I messed up."

When they caught up with her, she infected over 200 men by herself.

www.ingramcontent.com/pod-product-compliance
Lightning Source LLC
Chambersburg PA
CBHW070649120726
47909CB00004B/1641